The Woman with the Eggs

QUALITY TIME™ CLASSICS

TALES
OF
HANS CHRISTIAN ANDERSEN

The Little Match Girl
The Steadfast Tin Soldier
The Top and the Ball
The Woman with the Eggs

Library of Congress Cataloging-in-Publication Data

Erickson, Jon E.
  The woman with the eggs.

  (Quality time classics)
  Adaptation of: Konen med aeggene.
  Summary: A greedy woman is so preoccupied with her plans for becoming rich from selling her eggs that she forgets she is carrying them in a basket on her head.
  1. Children's poetry, American. [1. Danish poetry. 2. Eggs--Poetry] I. Andersen, H. C. (Hans Christian), 1805-1875. Konen med aeggene. II. Mogensen, Jan, ill. III. Title. IV. Series.
PS3555.R43W66 1987   811'.54   87-42583
ISBN 1-55532-344-8
ISBN 1-55532-319-7 (lib. bdg.)

This North American edition first published in 1987 by

Gareth Stevens, Inc.
7221 West Green Tree Road
Milwaukee, Wisconsin 53223, USA

First published as *Konen med aeggene* with an original copyright by Mallings, Copenhagen. This edition published by arrangement with Breakwater Books Limited, St. John's, Newfoundland.

Typeset by Web Tech, Inc., Milwaukee

2 3 4 5 6 7 8 9 92 91 90 89 88

The Woman with the Eggs

by Hans Christian Andersen

**retold in contemporary verse
by Jon Erickson**

illustrations by Jan Mogensen

Gareth Stevens Publishing
Milwaukee

There once was a woman who had a hen
That laid an egg each day, and then

She put a basket on her head,
And left for town with happy tread.

She dreamed of all the cash she'd make.
With all those coins, for goodness sake,

She'd buy *three* hens who'd start to lay,
And soon more folks would start to pay.

And from that cash *six* hens she'd own.
And half their eggs she'd hatch. When grown,

These hens would be her poultry farm.

"They'll make me cash, so what's the harm...

"I'll buy some geese and then a lamb —
Feathers and wool! How rich I am!

"I'll buy a pig and then a cow,
And maybe I'll get two, somehow.

"With all I earn, I'll servants keep
In a mansion surrounded by cows and sheep.

"A rich man will ask me to share his life —
I'll have me a husband, and he'll have a wife!

"He'll buy me a farm that is bigger than mine
So I'll grow proud and grand and fine.

"Folks will see me toss my head — "
And as these words were barely said,

She tossed her head! The eggs went SPLAT!

For all her dreams...Well, *that* was *that!*

THE END